DORCHADAS HOUSE

EMMANUELLE DE MAUPASSANT

Edited by
MELISSA COFFEY

First published in 2018

Cover design by Victoria Cooper

AUTHOR'S NOTE

IN WRITING DORCHADAS HOUSE, I was inspired by the suspenseful 'Gothic' novels of my teenage years: those by Daphne du Maurier, Victoria Holt and Mary Stewart.

The Scottish isle of Eirig is fictitious. Though its landscape is drawn from my recollections of visiting the Western Isles of the Outer Hebrides, its geography bears no resemblance to that of any of the actual islands. Likewise, the events of this story, alongside its characters, are the product of my imagination.

Readers may recognise some elements of Scottish (and English) folklore, which I have shamelessly reshaped, to create this flamboyant tale.

'Dorchadas House' is drawn from a short story I wrote in 2017, called 'The Ritual'.

PROLOGUE

THE BOAT APPROACHED the cliffs on the eastern side of the island. Sheer rock, softening into hills. Although I'd never been to Eirig, I felt a sense of familiarity. We journeyed on, until the harbour came into sight, a welcome calm after the choppiness of the open sea.

With its row of low stone cottages along the shore, and lobster creels on the jetty, Eirig was just as I'd imagined it would be, down to the tang of seaweed cast high upon the beach, decaying in the autumn sun, and the call of cormorants overhead.

Whatever I was, or had been, I would leave behind. My old self was like the waves which had moved beyond the boat, their crests becoming indistinct, dwindling in the distance.

I would forget, and there would be no one here to cause me to remember.

CHAPTER 1

WHAT WAS I HOPING FOR? To escape? From the young curate, simpering love poetry as he held my hand limply in his? From the butcher's son, smelling of blood? He'd taken me to the pictures once, pushing his hand under my skirt. All I could think of was the old meat lingering under his nails.

My mother had been an only child and my father not an Inverary-man. There was no-one to dispute my claim upon our house. A desirable property, looking across the harbour. It would bring a tidy sum.

'You shouldna be so picky,' my neighbour said. 'There's few enough men to choose from and plenty enough widows. All those soldiers lost in the war;

you'll have to take what ye can get, or you'll end up a spinster.'

Even in church there was no peace. Too many eyes, watching, judging, waiting for me to marry. My father was barely in his grave. He was unwell for so long I can hardly remember the man who daily saluted the calendar print of King George VI, framed upon the wall, and who took my mother dancing on a Saturday evening.

So many months of nursing him. Waking, he'd cry out for her.

'Don't worry, Da, she's resting next door,' I'd say. 'You'll see her soon.'

He'd whimper, from the pain, and I'd hold his hand.

'I'm here, Da.'

When he slept, I'd stand at the window, looking out. I made cups of tea that were cold by the time I thought to drink them. A shadow crept over me, and I'd think about the poison in the pantry cupboard. A spoonful in a dram of whisky would do it. He need drink only half. I felt the temptation, saw the danger, fought the compulsion that threatened to overtake me.

I told the doctor that he must have passed in the

night; I'd found him cold, taking up his kipper that last morning.

Whatever guilt I felt, I tempered it with knowledge of my many months of care. He'd been forced into intimacies with me that no man should endure from a woman not his wife. It had shamed him at first, and he'd clutched at the covers when I came to wash him. By the end, he barely knew what I did for him.

In the days that followed, I looked for grief to arrive, for tears, or anger. I loved him, didn't I? Instead, I was relieved. I'd been set free.

Inverary is a pretty place, with its white-washed town houses looking down the loch, but I could think only of leaving. To go where, I couldn't say. I took out the map and looked at the names. I'd never been to Glasgow. I wondered how I might like to live there. The anonymity of a city appealed to me, but I doubted I could bear the noise, or the dirt, or the crowds upon the street.

It was in that mood, of indecisive determination, that I saw the advertisement in the Hebridean Chronicle.

Personal assistant sought to help in the running of

Dorchadas House, on the island of Eirig: a retreat for women of an independent mind.

Eirig. It's sheep the place is known for, mostly, out on the hills. There would be space to think. In going where I was unknown, I might discover who it was I wanted to be. I took up my pen to apply, and Mrs McInnes replied within the fortnight.

Dorchadas House is quite grand. A sheltered spot, with a walled garden. Twenty bedrooms, though only a handful in use. We envisage attracting women writers and artists, and those who enjoy the outdoor life, who will take pleasure in exploring Eirig's remote, natural beauty.

Beyond that provided by the house's oil-fuelled generator, Mrs McInnes' letter explained, Eirig had no electricity. The postal office had the telegraph, but no telephone line. The packet boat came once a week with deliveries.

I was to begin on the first of the new month, with accommodation and meals provided, and a modest wage. My duties were reasonable. Only occasional cooking, and no cleaning. There were women from the village for that, and men for the heavy work. I'd oversee the decoration of the bedrooms. New wall-papers had been ordered. There were several hand-weavers on the island, making cloth for bedspreads and curtains. One thing they were not short of was wool. The old crafts might be dying on the main-land, but the peddle looms still had their place on Eirig.

The main part of my work would come later: placing invitations in the relevant periodicals, to entice suitable guests, organizing the boat to take them to and fro, from Oban. I'd manage the book-ings, and see that our visitors had everything to ensure their comfort. I'd be an assistant to Mrs McInnes, in running the house.

If I found myself unsuited to island life, she assured me I'd be free to leave with a month's notice.

There was little I regretted leaving behind. My clothes fitted into two small cases and I wore the heaviest: a green sweater and good quality skirt of brown tweed, which had been my mother's. My winter coat had been hers too. With my stoutest shoes, and my beret, scarf and gloves, I was ready to face whatever the Western Isles had in store for me.

The boat met me as agreed, at Inverary Harbour, smelling strongly of fish. It was, like its captain, salt-ravaged by the waves and wind. Buchanan introduced himself, tying to the pier only long enough for me to step on board. There was no one to see me off, but he said nothing of it, nodding to the stern as he took my bag.

'Sit ye inside. The sea's a wee bit rough, but we'll manage. Ye'll not be sick I hope.'

I'd not travelled beyond the loch before, never into the open sea. No matter if I were to be sick, I was heading to Eirig and I thrilled to the thought of it. As Inverary grew smaller behind us, the burden of so much I'd carried eased, blown by the breeze pushing us out with the tide. From the boat, the hills were more magnificent, and the birds' cries more piercing, as if my ears and eyes had come alive, and wished to take in everything anew.

Leaving behind the mouth of the loch, the boat heaved and rolled, but it was not as bad as I'd feared.

'Look at the horizon, lassie,' Captain Buchanan had advised. 'There's a blanket there for ye, and a flask. It'll be some four hours to reach Eirig, and I'll drop the creels as we go. The crab are good this season.'

He said little more on the journey, only pointing out the jagged tops of the Cuillins, on the distant Isle of Skye, as we travelled south-west. Once we were on the wildest expanse of the Minch, I did my best to hold on, and not be sent sprawling.

I was glad of the blanket and the sweet cocoa, for the damp of the sea air penetrated my coat too easily. By the time the outline of Eirig appeared, the chill was in my bones.

Nevertheless, my heart leapt to see Eirig's cliffs come into sight, violet dark, with the sun sinking to touch them. The past was a distant land and this, my new home.

CHAPTER 2

CAPTAIN BUCHANAN LIFTED my bags ashore and nodded to a horse-drawn trap waiting.

'My girl, Mhairi, will take you up to the house.'

Stroking the nose of the horse was a young woman, wrapped tight in a shawl over her dark dress. She watched as I walked unsteadily, my legs still in motion with the sea.

'It's kind of you to come,' I said, wishing to start off on a good foot. She was about my own age; there was the possibility of friendship.

'Mrs McInnes sent me,' she replied, implying that she wouldn't have bothered if the choice had been her own.

'Thank you, nonetheless.'

I returned her coolness with what I hoped was a

disarming smile. 'I'm Iris, and very pleased to meet you.'

She had the grace to lend me her hand as I stepped up to sit on the trap. There were few motor vehicles in Inverary; perhaps none here.

'I like your coat,' said Mhairi, her eyes appraising my attire.

Her tone was wistful rather than envious. Her own clothing was serviceable but drab, her skirt much longer than was fashionable.

'Let's get going then,' she said, rising to join me.

We set off on a fair track, leading from the harbour, southwards, the sea to our left. Mhairi pulled an apple from her pocket and offered it to me but I shook my head. I was hungry, but there would be a supper for me at the house, I felt sure.

She shrugged and took a bite herself.

There were a great many sheep grazing, hardly lifting their heads as we passed, intent on their grassy meal. Those on the track shuffled out of the way as we approached, looking indignant rather than afraid.

'Do you have sheep yourself?' I asked, eager to engage her in conversation.

'A few. It's what we mostly do here: raise sheep. They go to market at the end of the summer. My Da and the others take them on their boats. We keep the best for tupping, o' course.'

'Tupping?'

'When we let the ram at the ewes! Don't you know anything?'

I blushed, from the embarrassment of ignorance rather than from prudery. I'd have to learn more of farming ways.

'But your father fishes?' I answered, thinking it best to turn the conversation.

'Aye, though he can only go to sea, if the weather permits. 'Tis been a good few months for the crab and lobster, and the langoustine. Those fetch the best prices in Oban. Some o' the others fish regular, with nets. There's a smokehouse up at Dorchadas, where they hang the mackerel and haddock.'

She paused to take a bite of the apple.

'There's the orchard too, o'course, behind the big house. They sell a few but we mostly eat these'ns ourselves. Mrs McInnes makes a good cider.'

I listened to the steady creak of the trap's wheels turning, and the rhythm of the horse's hooves. Grazing sheep glowed pale in the mauve twilight.

'Do you have children?'

As soon as it was out of my mouth I regretted it. I hated to be asked personal questions, or for others to make assumptions about me, as to whether I should be married, or how I should be conducting myself.

Mhairi seemed happy to answer, however.

'O aye, I've a bairn three years old. He's right bonny. I keep house for my father, and it suits us right enough. My mother and younger brother passed, so it's just us now.'

She flicked the reins to urge on the horses.

I couldn't help but notice her left hand, and the wedding band that wasn't there.

'I don't need a husband,' she said curtly, seeing my glance. 'I'm happy as I am.' She looked sideways at me, her eyes mischievous. 'I can get what I need from men without being married to one.' She shook her hair behind her, as if to emphasize her carefree state.

Where I'd nursed resentment at being judged for my spinsterhood, Mhairi was at ease in hers. An impulse to laugh rose in me and came out in a bark, which made her stare in surprise.

'You an' me might get along,' said Mhairi.

She'd bitten her apple down to the pips, which she spat into the verge.

CHAPTER 3

I<small>T WASN'T LONG</small> before the track curved inland and the wind dropped as we found shelter between the hills. The moon had risen, full-silvered, a gleaming eye peering down upon our little cart.

Where the coastal road had been alive with the shriek of gannets and cormorants, here there were no bird calls. The corncrake and nightjar had flown to warmer climes, autumn being upon us. Still, it seemed strange not to hear a single cry, not even from some hunting owl.

I felt neither a shiver, nor an ache, but something between. A feeling of anticipation, I told myself; I was soon to see the household in which I'd be living.

Even Mhairi had fallen silent, her eyes upon the track, which bent almost upon itself, before rising gently upwards, between an expanse of shadowy trees. After some minutes, we emerged, met by moonlight and an open sky in which the stars were now visible. Being a high place, the wind was stronger here, sweeping across the expanse of gorse and scattered rock.

There was a dark mass upon the summit, one I couldn't discern clearly. Not the house, for there were no lights.

'What is it?' My voice seemed loud under that great sky.

'It's the circle.'

'Inside, o' course,' she added. 'You can't see it 'til you're inside.'

It was an answer that made no sense to me. I knew only that my chest had begun to pound, and I held Mhairi's arm until we'd passed.

CHAPTER 4

THE TRACK SWUNG about again and began to descend, until it brought Dorchadas House into view. What a grand residence it must have been, with its great columns, and tall windows looking across the wild heathland, to the night twinkle of the sea. The stonework of the terrace balustrade had begun to crumble, and several windows were cracked, if not broken. Were it not to fall into further disrepair, money would be needed.

There was but one light, which travelled from a room to the right of the porch, coming closer, until it disappeared from view, and the oak door opened.

The bearer of the lamp was Mrs McInnes. Handsome and of uncommon height, she was perhaps in her early forties, though she dressed as one far older, her chestnut hair worn severely in a bun, and wearing a dress of plain serge.

'Good evening, Miss Muir, and thank you, Mhairi. Will you stay in the little bedroom off the kitchen? I've enough supper for you.'

'I will,' replied Mhairi, before I'd a chance to return Mrs McInnes' greeting. 'I've left the bairn with Flora's mother for the night.'

'Take the horse round to the stables then. The boys will attend to him, and will be glad to see you, I'm sure…'

By the light of the lantern, I could see the hallway was large; I could only guess at how far back it reached, for the illumination did not reach to its corners. A magnificent staircase ascended, soaring into the darkness.

'You've trouble with the generator, Mrs McInnes?'

Her expression was neutral, though her eyes narrowed.

'We must make economies, Miss Muir, for the sake of our venture. The money I'm saving on the fuel has paid for our Edinburgh wallpapers, which are soon to arrive.'

She smiled, somewhat brusquely.

'Only a few rooms downstairs are wired in any case. The Laird is against installing electricity, as we've managed so many years without. It was his wife who persuaded him to have the generator, so that the dining room, library and kitchen might be lit.'

It will be as it was when I was a little girl, I thought, just after the Great War.

'You'll need a lamp to take you to bed, but I believe they'd call it romantic, in Glasgow, or London, to rely on the old ways.'

Holding the lantern high, Mrs McInnes led me to the back of the hall, and we made our way along a chill corridor. There was a strong smell of damp, overlaid with that of cooking.

'You're hungry, I expect,' she said.

The kitchen was a good size, with a well-blacked stove, and bread ovens to either side. Upon the top sat a pot of soup: the source of the appetizing aroma.

'Mrs Cameron has made Cullen Skink. We smoke the fish ourselves and the milk for the broth is fresh from the ewes this morning. You'll eat better here than you did in Inverary, I shouldn't wonder.'

Taking a bowl, she ladled a good amount, and cut a hunk of bread to go with it. She did not sit, but busied herself in filling the kettle, to heat upon the stove.

'We have all we need, Miss Muir, though perhaps our needs are modest.'

Filled generously with haddock and herring, the soup was delicious.

'The boiler burns both wood and peat. There's enough water for one bath each evening, Miss Muir, so you may let me know which days you prefer.'

She lifted the kettle, which had begun to whistle, pouring its contents into the pot.

'We rely still on our hearths to warm the house. We don't bother in the summer months, of course, but it's drawing chill now that October's with us.'

Mrs McInnes filled our cups.

'Shona and Margaret set the fires every morning. I ask that you don't light the kindling unless you intend to remain in a room.'

I could see that I'd be glad of my worsted stockings!

'We've a stream that flows past the house, from which we draw the water, so you may find it silty on occasion.' She took a sip from her cup. 'We've a well for the drinking water, of course.'

I managed a wan smile.

'Thank you, Mrs McInnes. And the soup was wonderful.'

'You're very welcome, my dear. Now, finish your tea. It's nettle, red clover and raspberry leaf: good for the blood. Then, I think an early night is in order.'

Gratefully, I followed her back to the hallway, armed with my own lantern. Someone had taken my bags up the stairs. On entering my room, I found that the fire was lit, and the guard placed about it; the smell of peat was heavy but not unpleasant.

'Sleep well, my dear,' said Mrs McInnes. 'We shall talk more in the morning.'

With that, she closed the door and I sat on the edge of the bed. The room contained a small armchair, a wardrobe, dressing table and chest of drawers. They were all of good oak. Someone had placed sprigs of heather in a vase.

A terrible tiredness came over me, such that I wished only to kick off my shoes and climb into bed. I went to draw the curtains, from habit, if not necessity. The moon, which had shone so brightly, was now covered by clouds.

EVEN ON THAT FIRST NIGHT, I dreamt. A presence, in

the darkness. Under its gaze, my skin burned and I felt the swell of fear. It called to me, to the darkness within myself.

I awoke to the room's chill, licked by the first hint of winter's tongue, and the feeling retreated, to some hidden place.

CHAPTER 5

THE COOK, Mrs Cameron, was up to her elbows in flour as I entered the kitchen, cheeks ruddy with the exertion of kneading the dough for her bannock loaves. She nodded at me.

'Good morning, Miss Muir. You've arrived safely, I see.'

'Your soup, last night, was most welcome, Mrs Cameron. The tastiest I've eaten.'

The compliment was well-received. There are few cooks, I know, who can resist the pleasure of having their efforts praised.

'You're most welcome. Now, sit ye down. I've the porridge ready. You've just missed Mhairi. She was up with the dawn to drive back to her wee bairn.

Mrs McInnes will join you shortly. She's checking on the smokehouse, I believe.'

'She's a very dutiful housekeeper,' I ventured. The bowl set before me steamed. 'My room's spotless, and the sheets so white.'

Mrs Cameron sniffed. 'Of course, she doesn't clean anything herself. Shona and Margaret do that, and Flora the linens. Mhairi helps out, sometimes.'

I nodded. A house as large as this needed staff, even if most of it was shut up.

'And I'd not be referring to her as the housekeeper.' Mrs Cameron added, thumping the dough onto the table. 'She's been here a long time, and thinks of herself as kin to the Laird, or as close as can be...'

'What's the Laird like?' I asked. 'Will I meet him today?'

I saw Mrs Cameron's face close.

'He keeps to his rooms, and lives quietly. He's been unwell this past nine months.'

I expressed my regret at hearing this news.

'Mrs McInnes keeps him company and takes his meals to him, though he hasn't much of an appetite. 'Twill be both a sadness and a gift when he passes.'

She paused in working the bread.

'It will be a sorrowful time, I've no doubt,' I answered. For a moment, I saw the day of my own father's funeral. Standing in the rain, as the coffin was lowered. I didn't want to think of it.

'Does he leave an heir, to take over the estate?'

Mrs Cameron stopped her work to speak.

'The Laird hasn't been backward in planting his seed. Before his illness, he was strong and handsome. Likely there are few on the island not descended from the great lairds of Tigh Dorchadas.'

I sat, red in the cheek, unsure whether to apologize for my nosiness, or to pretend nothing had been said. I'd read enough novels to know how the aristocracy behaved. Novels, I've always thought, hold as much truth in them as make-believe.

The back door to the kitchen opened and Mrs McInnes entered, holding a clutch of fish upon a string.

'Mackerel for lunch, Mrs Cameron,' she said, placing them onto a platter beside the sink.

'It's a bonny day. You should ken the island a little better, Miss Muir. Breathe its air. Let it enchant you.'

She took a seat at the trestle table.

'There are carrots to be pulled in the garden, if you'd be so kind. When you come back, we'll sit in my parlour with some of Mrs Cameron's gingerbread and discuss our plans.'

I rose, eager to act on her suggestion.

Mrs McInnes looked up at me.

'And you should see our maze, Miss Muir, at the summit of the hill.'

SUMMER HAD ENDED, but something of its comfort remained, the air warmer than could be expected for October. Looking across the hillside, towards the sea, I was filled with an urge to run and leap. I did just that, until I was breathless, and climbed onto a rock to admire the view. Eirig was a wild place, always in motion, from the distant, frothing waves to the long grass, rippling. I let the wind move over my skin. It was impossible to feel grief, or regret. I was aware only of being gloriously alive.

I felt the openness of the landscape, as a bird must feel its freedom from the cage. The narrow house and narrow life of Inverary held no sway over me now. I had only to close my eyes and the heaviness of my memories lifted. However, as I stood there, I felt the prickle upon my neck of being watched, though there were only the sheep, steadily munching, raising their heads merely to look about for the next tuft of green.

I looked upwards, to where Mrs McInnes had

indicated the maze was situated. I was breathless by the time I reached the top, having had little opportunity to walk the hills about Inverary. Here was the dark mass that had disquieted me the night before: a tall hedge stretching wide in either direction. An impenetrable wall, except that there was an opening before me, an arch in the yew, just wide enough to allow entry.

I thought I heard someone. It was a soft echo of a whisper, spoken into the slip of air, breathed through the hedge and into my ear. Someone speaking my name.

'Iris ... Iris.'

'Who's there?' I said. 'Who are you?'

Who could it be? Mhairi? Mrs Cameron had told me she'd returned to the village. It must only be the wind, playing tricks.

I stepped inside, and all was still. I took the passage before me, listening, and heard it again, that gentle whisper. I pushed my cheek to the yew. There it was: low and seductive, a call which brought a winding shiver through my body. I wandered, drawn deeper, travelling the veins of the maze, the voice growing quiet, then returning, leading me onwards, into the heart of that place.

I continued, back and forth, and around, until the

hedge revealed an open space: a wide clearing with a stone at its centre. Naught else. The voice which had so enchanted and enticed me was silent, and yet something was here. Something.

Swollen-bellied, like a woman with child, the stone reached to the height of my waist. It was flat on top, with a hole in the middle. I crouched to look closer, slid my palm around the smooth opening, reached my fingers inwards.

Would I fit?

I wanted to. It was large enough, I was sure. I sat back and removed my coat. Yes, I'd fit. I could wriggle through and out the other side. I'd spent too many years being sensible. Now, if I wanted to do a thing, I'd do it.

The squeeze was tight, but I managed, arms followed by shoulders. At my hips, the stone formed a tight ring about my pelvis, but then my legs slithered through, and I was reminded of a foal being born from its mother, deposited in ungainly fashion upon the ground. At last, I stood upright on the other side, resting my back against the hard surface.

An adder crept from beneath the stone, eyes like black dewdrops, watching me, before pouring itself away down a crevice.

Only then did I notice the others, four or five feet

apart, and of various sizes. Stones forming a complete circle, pressed close into the hedge, almost hidden in the yew.

I'd seen a photograph of something similar at Callanish, on the west coast of the Isle of Lewis, and read of other circles, on Orkney, though those stones were much larger.

There were stories about such places. Human sacrifices? Or perhaps it was just lambs they offered up... slitting their throats and letting the blood form a libation, the rich liquid soaking into the soil beneath the sacred centre stone.

I stepped away from where I'd been leaning.

Just stories, and just stones.

Nevertheless, I felt a twinge of disquiet. I put on my coat and hurried back the way I'd come. I no longer wanted to be there.

CHAPTER 6

WALKING BACK TOWARDS THE HOUSE, the distance wasn't far at all and I wondered at it having seemed so. I became aware of the windows. So many, looking down at me. Empty rooms, of course, though Mrs Cameron and Mrs McInnes were in there somewhere, and the others: little worker ants brushing the ash from each grate before laying the fire anew, dusting furniture, and passing laundry through the mangle.

They might pause in their work to look out at me, but it was unlikely. Everyone was occupied in this house. Too busy to idly gaze across the heath.

I remembered the carrots; the vegetable garden must be at the back. I took the path to the side of the house, where Mhairi had driven her trap the night before. Sure enough, there were stables, the doors half open, to allow the horses air. Four sleek heads turned to look at me as I passed, snorting and mane-shaking. I'd never learnt to ride a horse but perhaps I would, while I was here. It would be marvellous to gallop across the open landscape, feeling the wind in my hair.

Further on was a barn, the door ajar. I paused, curious to look in, and heard a squeal, and a man's voice, cursing.

There were two of them inside the stall, wrestling a ram to the ground, pinning it on its back.

'What are you doing? You're not hurting it, are you?'

Their heads were lowered, faces hidden beneath hair thick and curling. As they looked up, I felt the blood come to my face. They were brothers, for sure, as alike as two men can be. Each was broad shoul-dered, with arms used to manual work. Some days had passed since they'd shaved, as their chins were ginger-stubbled. Dishevelled as they were, they radi-ated health and physical strength.

'Ah, it's our Inverary-Miss,' said one. 'Come to learn our farming ways. Tip your hat, Eachainn, to our lady from the grand town.'

He grinned, giving a mock dip of his head.

'I'm here to help Mrs McInnes,' I said. 'And I don't think she'd be pleased to hear of you being rude to me…'

'Is that the way of it?' said the first, hauling the ram closer between his legs. He held it firm, and it stopped struggling, as if sensing when it was beaten.

'If you want to know, we're checking for sheep scab,' said the one named Eachainn. 'And good teeth and feet.'

'And firm testicles.'

The pair looked at one another and exchanged a smile.

'Do you ken how to check for those, lassie?'

'An experienced ram will manage at least eighty ewes. You need good bollocks on you for that, eh, Neas!' He gripped his own, and grinned lewdly at me.

'There's no need to be vulgar,' I said, turning away.

Men! Always thinking they could say what they liked. And all the time looking at you as if your only purpose was to be tipped into bed; or into the hay, in the case of these two.

'On you go, lassie,' said Neas, waving his arm dismissively. 'Take your fine town nose out of here, but don't say we didn't offer to teach you.'

I gritted my teeth. I disliked being mocked, but

wanted to show my willingness. They'd accept me sooner, I hoped.

'Come here, lassie, and we'll show you,' said Eachainn, in a placatory fashion. 'You can hardly live on Eirig and not know what's what.'

I stepped closer.

'You'll need to climb over,' said the other, with a smirk. 'To get a proper look. We'll show you something useful, if you're willing.'

It wasn't difficult to navigate the bars of the stall, though less than ladylike. They watched as I did so, swinging my leg over the top and descending with as much grace as I could muster.

'Nicely done,' said Eachainn, with a lazy smile. He patted the straw beside him. 'Now, lassie, come ye here.'

I went to stand beside him,

'First thing is the toes.' Eachainn splayed the ram's clews as he spoke. 'There should be no bad smell or heat in the foot. Cannae have any lameness when there's a whole flock want tupping!'

'Kneel down, lass,' said the other. 'You want to look closer.'

I did so reluctantly, fearing that the ram would kick me, but did as they directed, taking up a position near its head.

'Next is the teeth.' He pulled back the ram's gums. 'You need to see a good bite, and none missing.' He took my hand and pressed it to the ram's cheek. 'Feel for swelling, which could indicate disease.'

The ram lay surprisingly still as I stroked its face, though its eyes rolled in its head. I began to feel ashamed of myself. However uncouth, these men knew their work.

'Now,' said Eachainn, 'The most important part: the scrotum!'

He uttered the word with relish. Seizing the base, he rolled the flesh between thumb and forefinger, his eyes flicking upwards to assess my composure. Despite my discomfort, I found that I did not wish to look away.

'The testicles should move easily within the sac,' said the other, his eyes glinting with mischief, 'which should be free of sores or injuries.'

'What do you think, lassie?' said Neas. 'Will this one pass muster?'

I nodded my head curtly, refusing to rise to the provocation.

Eachainn continued, moving his fingers to explore the ram's genitals. 'At the base of the scrotum is what's called the epididimus, see? 'Bout the size of a walnut.'

'Where semen is stored,' said his brother, giving me a wink. 'Give me your hand, lassie, and I'll help you find it!'

He reached for my fingers but I snatched them away, my cheeks flaring.

'All seems in order,' said Eachainn, smirking at my disquiet. 'Ready for the job!'

'Just the tossle, now.' Neas leant forward, and pulled to extrude the ram's penis.

In comparison to the huge testicles, the appendage looked a sorry thing, no broader than a worm.

'She's a country lass at heart,' said Eachainn, rising to slap his brother on the back. 'Can't resist a good look!'

'Don't be disappointed for the ewes, lass; it's big enough to do what's needed. Nature's design is all it should be.'

They let go of the ram, which flipped over swiftly, kicking up its feet and tossing its head, bleating somewhat defiantly.

'Thank you for that. Most instructional. Now, you'll excuse me,' I said, deciding that a brusque tone was necessary. 'I've some vegetables to pull.'

'You're most welcome, lass,' called Eachainn. 'You can climb over again if you like. We'll both enjoy the view.' He folded his arms and nodded towards the gate in the corner. 'Or you can lift the latch, like we did, when we came in.'

Neas threw back his head in laughter and I cursed them both beneath my breath as I walked away.

CHAPTER 7

I WAS AWARE, always, of the maze upon the hill, and the strange stones within. Even out of sight of its dark walls, I felt a presence, and the pull of that place, inviting me to return. I told myself it was a childish obsession, and fought to distract myself.

Before the supper was set, I'd go out to enjoy the soft fall of evening. The breeze blew the long grasses flat, and sent violet clouds scudding, cracks of gold appearing with the lowering sun. If I stayed very still, I'd see a hare darting from the gorse, its white scat bright in the half-light. I took every opportunity to walk the open heath. I wished to be alone, listening for the warbling of a thrush, enjoying the freshness on my face.

Neas and Eachainn, for all their physical prowess, were brutish. I contrived to avoid them, as far as I was able. At mealtimes, they would find ways to touch me. Their gaze was arrogant: that of men who know themselves strong, and desired by women.

Shona and Margaret would find any excuse to go out to the barn. I saw them from the kitchen window, squealing at the approach of a groping hand, yet making little attempt to remove themselves from reach. Whatever lewd comments passed their way, they seemed to take as compliments.

I endeavoured to concentrate on my duties, and to familiarize myself with the house. Stretching back from each end was a small wing, East and West. Both were in disrepair. Mrs Cameron bemoaned the use of her pots to catch water from one part of the leaking roof. We were to concentrate on the main building for our renovations. There would be time for the rest when finances permitted.

I opened doors, disturbing dust. So many rooms, long unused. I sat at dressing tables and lay on beds. Looking in a mottled mirror, I looked at my own face, and the dark swathe of my hair. I imagined the women who'd done so before me. All those faces, and bodies, now dust themselves. I'd peer beyond the familiar gaze of my own hazel eyes, probing the shadows behind me, in those antiquated rooms, with their peeling wallpapers and faded tapestries. I half hoped some phantom would materialise. Fancying a footfall behind me, or the swish of silk, I enjoyed seeing how far I might scare myself.

'Avoid the East Wing,' Mrs McInnes said. 'It's where the Laird's rooms are located, and he wishes to see and hear no-one. He's not long for this world, and has earned the right to a peaceful end.'

In the night, I'd listen. When the wind was still, I felt every sigh of air. Quiet steps. Sometimes, a creaking hinge. Low voices, and someone crying, I thought, but far away, as if on the heath, or an echo in the walls, from another time, in the space between wakefulness and sleep.

One night, there was a great, howling wind, relentless, sweeping the outer walls. The wind pulled at me, refusing to let me sleep. I understood, then, where the legend of the Scottish Banshees originated. Something in me wanted to howl too. To throw open the window and let all that wild energy fill the room. Perhaps, I'd be blown away: sucked out and thrown into the air, to fly over the heath.

I ADMIRED MRS MCINNES. Like myself, she was a

woman alone, and managing well without a husband. She spoke without flattery or offence and, most importantly, treated me as her equal.

Together, we drew up a plan for the restoration of the house. There was a modest pot of money to begin our project, which we would direct in making the bedrooms comfortable, and in installing a bathroom on the upper floor. A plumber and glazier were to come from the mainland, to extend the hot water piping from the kitchen, and to mend several cracked panes of glass. Neas and Eachainn, being used to turning their hand to all manner of work, would begin repointing the stonework, as far as they were able, and would be sent onto the roof to replace lost tiles.

A small budget had been set aside for advertisements. We would place them in early Spring, inviting residents to arrive on the island just as the weather turned warmer. As soon as bookings began, the coffers would swell, and other work could commence.

We chatted amiably as we hung new wallpapers in the bedrooms, and took down old curtains. Mrs McInnes' sewing machine was kept busy, transforming the cloth woven on Eirig looms into new drapes and cushions and coverlets for the beds. I sewed by hand what could not be done on the machine. Our female guests might lack hot water radiators and electric lighting in their rooms, but they would be cozy enough.

I avoided raising topics of a personal nature, having no wish to recall the drudgery of my life in Inverary. I knew Mrs McInnes would share details of her own past if and when she was ready. We spoke instead of the house's history, and of the island.

Dorchadas House had been built in the seventeenth century, and the maze, in which I had wandered, was planted at that time. Mrs McInnes had no idea of the age of the stones, but it was common knowledge that the first Laird Dorchadas, given the estate by King Charles II himself for his support in the restoration of the crown, had been fascinated by the 'old ways'.

'Paganism?' I asked. 'Appeasing the spirits of nature?'

'Yes, lassie. That sort of thing…' she replied, sucking on a thread to enable its passing through her needle.

'And the maze?' I enquired. 'Why did he plant it around the circle?'

'For privacy, perhaps. There are other stories, of

the ceremonies performed by the first laird,' said Mrs McInnes. 'We can only imagine… wicked debauchery, no doubt! You know your Gaelic a little, don't you, lassie?'

I nodded.

'Tigh Dorchadas is our own 'House of Darkness'. Some folk say the devil himself dances in the maze on nights of the new moon.'

Her eyes gleamed mischievously.

'Of course, only those brave enough to venture out can say for sure!'

She chuckled, and I smiled coyly in return. I was a little shocked, but I found her manner refreshing.

The largest of the sitting rooms, along with the dining room, was a little faded in its grandeur, but impressive enough, and sure to appeal to the romantic nature of our prospective guests. Their wallpapers were all of darker hues, in green and burgundy, interspersed with paintings of stags, horses and dogs. There were the customary land-scapes, and several maritime scenes of boats tossed on wild seas.

The family portraits included one of the Laird, seated beside his wife and young child. He appeared most handsome, wearing his kilt and ruffled shirt. His hair, luxuriously thick, curled in the true Scottish ginger hue. His wife was pale-complexioned, with delicate wrists and fine features; the child favoured her fair looks rather than those of his father.

'And how is the Laird?' I asked, as Mrs McInnes took me through the reception rooms. 'Mrs Cameron mentioned that he's been unwell.'

Mrs McInnes lowered her eyes. 'I do my best to make him comfortable. 'Tis a sorrowful thing to see him brought so low. Any man of lesser constitution would have since passed into the next life. It would be for the best, perhaps, for to linger in pain is a sore trial to a man once great.'

I expressed my regret at this, knowing only too well the degradation of such an end. I recalled my own father's final weeks, no longer able to speak, or take nourishment, his eyes barely seeing me.

'And his son?' I asked. 'Away to study on the mainland?'

Mrs McInnes shook her head. 'He was a sickly thing and such as he don't last long in this world. He wasn't the sort to thrive on a place like Eirig. Strong blood's what's needed.'

I wondered again who would become the next laird, whether an heir had been nominated.

'In his youth, the Laird was a fine figure of a

man,' declared Mrs McInnes. 'As attractive as any woman could wish for, and not ungenerous in his attentions.'

She led me away from the portrait, to observe the view from the window. Neas and Eachainn were replacing the gate in the ram's pen, making sure the beast might not escape and bother the ewes before the official time of tupping.

'With his poor wife so often unwell in her bed,' she continued, 'we can hardly blame him for looking elsewhere. Several of the young men and women in the village have the look of him, as you may notice, when you know us better...'

It was a rather indelicate subject, which I chose not to pursue, although I was curious as to whom might now inherit the title, not to mention the house and land. Mrs McInnes appeared to be running everything, and to have full access to the finances of the estate. I resolved to ask again when I knew her better, not wishing to seem impertinent.

As the days passed, I came to love the sight of Eirig's sturdy sheep and shaggy Highland cows, which wandered freely over the island. Although the house boasted a fine vegetable garden, protected from the wind by its own wall, such crops were in limited supply on the island, as Mrs McInnes explained.

'October may be a rich month for camomile and barley harvests across the British Isles, but, here, we live with tufted grass and gorse,' she instructed me. 'Our crops thrive only in sheltered places, where the land is low-lying, and at the foot of our hills, where rainwater keeps the soil moist, fertilized by streams carrying sediment down the hillsides.'

We were sitting together in her parlour one evening, as had become our habit. The fire was lit, and the room comfortable, while the wind whipped against the window. I commented on the changing season as Mrs McInnes served her special tea.

'The wheel of the year is turning,' she remarked. 'Seeds have fallen deep, and must lie unseen until Spring comes again, but not all life is dormant. The sheep's bellies will be swelling now that we've begun the tupping. Our women too, tend to carry their babes over the winter months.'

She offered me a slice of Mrs Cameron's shortbread.

'Naturally, if we wish to reap the bounty of the land, we must pay our dues. The islanders used to sacrifice their children, you know, as well as milk and their best ewes. Tributes to appease the old gods. Nature is bountiful, but also destructive, Miss Muir. Winter brings darkness and blight, so we must do what we can to keep ourselves safe.'

As she refilled my cup, I wondered what the islanders chose for their sacrifice in these modern times.

'We'll soon be celebrating Samhain, it being the end of the growing season. The frosts are coming, so we'll choose which livestock to slaughter, and which to keep over the winter months. There's only so much fodder to feed them. The rest the boats will take to the mainland, for sale.'

'You're always so busy, Mrs McInnes, and you manage everything so well.'

She took the compliment with a modest nod of her head.

'I'd not manage at all were it not for the girls helping, of course,' she conceded. 'And my lovely boys. Neas and Eachainn are strong young men.'

She looked me in the eye.

'They'll make good fathers of children.'

I could hardly reply without causing offence. I'd no desire to marry, however, and not to such as Neas or Eachainn McInnes.

'They're handsome young men, and you must be proud,' I said, wishing to assuage her maternal desire to hear well of her sons.

'Like their father,' she replied, with a quiet smile.

DESPITE MY AVERSION to the charms of Mrs McInnes' sons, I thought of them while in my bed, indulging in night-fantasies that required no tenderness from a devoted lover. I imagined myself visiting the barn, where they would pin me, as they had the ram, obliging me to submit to their crude hands. Some nights, my dreams took me back to the maze. They pursued me through its passageways, until we reached the centre, where they laid me upon the stone, and I was powerless against the strength of their arms, and the weight of them.

I drifted to sleep with the smell of men unwashed, faces rough against my skin, and bodies hungry to consume me. I hated myself, yet was powerless against the fevered play of my desires.

CHAPTER 8

I'D FAILED to attend church the previous Sunday, having been en route to Eirig, and found that I slept late on the morning of the next. I rose hurriedly, doing my best with my hair. Though plaited at night, its waves were apt to tangle. I rolled most of the length at the nape of my neck, and the rest either side, above my ears, pinning hastily. I might have missed breakfast, I realised, and would have to do without. The kirk, I supposed, must be in the village, and some drive away. I'd no wish to detain the family and make them late. I made my way down as quickly as I could, carrying my Bible under my arm.

However, though the hour was close to nine, no-one was gathered in the hall. I found Mrs McInnes in her parlour, with the fire lit, a pot of tea beside her. Against the flames, she had a slice of bread toasting, and her hands were busy with her knitting.

'Very smart!' she remarked, seeing me in my best dress, of a fine, dark blue wool. 'The colour suits the bloom of your complexion, my dear.' Her gaze lingered. 'You've an attractive figure, it must be said.'

I smiled self-consciously. 'Is the service not at ten?' I asked, still somewhat breathless from hurrying. 'Or do you have it later here?'

She set down her needles. 'There's no service, Miss Muir, being as there's no rector to officiate. Did I not tell ye?' She rose to take another cup from the cabinet and placed it next to her own, inviting me to sit. 'He died of flu, near two years ago. None has been sent to replace him, so we have no service to attend.'

Remote as Eirig was, and small of population, the news greatly surprised me. It must be some oversight on the part of the diocese. At the very least, a clergyman could have been sent on some schedule of rotation, I was sure.

'I'm sorry to hear that Mrs McInnes, and sad too, for the loss of your rector,' I said, hanging my coat upon the hook on the back of the door. I watched as she poured tea into my cup.

'Yes, very sad,' she agreed, then clapped her

hands, as if to dismiss the memory. 'Will you take a slice of toast, Miss Muir? We don't have the full breakfast until eleven on a Sunday, and then our main meal around four. We've a nice goose, plucked and prepared already.'

I nodded vaguely. 'But how do you worship?' I enquired, returning again to the subject.

Picking up her needles, she began casting on, with nimble fingers.

'Mrs McInnes?' I prompted.

For some moments, she continued her knitting as if she hadn't heard me. 'We do that in our own way.' She gave me a curt smile. 'In truth, I don't miss attending the kirk. Always such a draughty place.'

I couldn't imagine any Scottish woman of Mrs McInnes' generation not steeped in the desire to demonstrate religious fervour. It seemed unthinkable that she, or any of the islanders, did not find a way to attend church on a Sunday. However, it would do me little good to rile at her for this apparent lack of faith, and I couldn't conjure a priest to suit my own inclinations.

We sat for a while, the room quiet but for the crackle of the fire and the click of Mrs McInnes' needles. The garment grew steadily: a cardigan for a baby, I guessed. No doubt, one of the women from the village was expecting.

'You should go for a walk,' she said, at last. 'No need to sit here with me. See where your feet take you.'

I went to change my shoes and set out, feeling unsettled still at Mrs McInnes' attitude. Were the distance not so great, I might have walked to the church myself, to sit quietly in a pew, and offer my own silent prayers. Since my father's passing I'd felt, more than ever, the need for sacred communion, for my own quiet confession of my sins, and the asking of forgiveness. I had tried so hard to be a dutiful daughter, but I had failed in ways known only to myself, and to God.

Consumed by these thoughts, I took the cliff path, being told that it was only about half a mile, and that I'd not lose my way. I had only to follow the downward slope of the cliffs and I'd be sure to find the shoreline. There was a pretty cove, she said, on which grey seals came to birth their pups in mid-September. If I were lucky, I might yet see them basking.

The sunshine was with me, making it a pleasant few hours. I made my way through the machair, lamenting that I'd arrived too late to see it in bloom.

However, even the spent seedheads made an enchanting sight, protruding from the sandy soil above the beach. I found a spot in the dunes surrounding the cove and settled to watch the young seals at play. They were already losing their fur, and becoming more active, wriggling at the water's edge, under the watchful eyes of their mothers.

The sea was at low tide, folding softly over itself, hushed in its gentle rhythm. I've always liked to listen to the sea. It's an eternal thing, to be relied upon. I find comfort in knowing that it will always be there, long after I am gone.

It was as I returned to the cliff path that I noticed the row of cottages on the headland. There were five of them, low and made from stone, their windows small and recessed. The thatch was in disrepair, though the netting holding it in place was still secure, weighted with large pebbles. They were positioned well for the view, although would have been exposed to any southerly wind.

The doors were unlocked. The first showed me enough, though it was so dark inside that it took time for my eyes to become accustomed. The box bed, surrounded on all sides by wooden panels, to keep out the night draught, still had a blanket upon it, and two yellowed pillows. The small bunk in the corner, in which the children must have slept, also had its bedding. Some mice had made a nest in the coverlet, leaving the faint smell of urine. Dried seathrift and grass had settled on the floor. A pan hung from a hook near the hearth, while six plates and bowls sat on the shelf. They were chipped and cracked; not worth taking, or someone would have done, I supposed.

What inspires a family to leave its home? Or obliges it?

Curious to know more of the history of this place, I walked around the cove, entering the cemetery. Perhaps two hundred graves, bounded by a wall, to keep the sheep from straying in. There was a small monument to fishermen lost at sea in 1879; another to those killed during the Great War. Each a modest list of names, but more than such a small island could afford to sacrifice. There would soon, perhaps, be a memorial to those lost in the recent war.

I passed among the smaller headstones; a few dated from the 1790s but many were more recent, the children stacked one upon the other underground much as they would have been in their beds, top to toe. It pulled at my heart to read the names, and the ages beside them.

Something had happened in 1947. At least thirty adults had been buried that year, and the same number of children. I recognized the names: McInnes, Cameron, Buchanan, Mackay, Stuart, and Muir. My own name.

CHAPTER 9

ON MY RETURN, I found Mhairi in the parlour. Mrs McInnes had taken the trap into the village, to pay some calls and Mhairi had walked up, wishing to use the sewing machine. The cast-off curtains from the bedrooms would make several dresses.

I made us a pot of tea and came to sit in the armchair, while Mhairi knelt on the floor, laying out the pattern from which she'd cut.

'You look at little peaky,' she remarked, removing a pin from her mouth.

I shrugged.

She continued working, cutting the panels of cloth.

'You've had a chance to explore?' she asked,

looking at me beadily. 'You've been through the house, and walked hereabouts?'

I told her then about what I'd seen: the cottages and the multitude of graves.

She hesitated before speaking, her fingers pleating the cloth.

'It was a bad business. We left the cottages as they were, it seeming wrong to touch anything. Besides which, it's bad luck to take from a house in which death has touched every person.'

'All of them?' I asked.

She sighed. 'We lost so many to the flu: old ones, but young too. Not that there were many children to begin with. Men had been away to fight, and not all returned.'

It was the same the country over; every town and village had lost good men. The news of an outbreak of flu on Eirig had passed me by, but I was no regular reader of newspapers. Still, I couldn't help but think of the Great Flu of 1918, though its sweep of death had ended before I was born.

'Was the doctor not able to help?' I asked.

'Dr McBane comes only once every three months. By the time he arrived, it was too late. The dead were long since in the next world.'

She looked at me, setting down the scissors to give me her attention.

'You saw the Muir graves?'

I nodded. It was on my lips to ask about the family name, to know more about them, but it was silly to imagine that they had anything to do with me. Muir is such a common Scottish name. Still, perhaps some of my ancestors might have been from Eirig. My father had moved to Inverary from the north, he'd said. My mother was an Inverary girl. It was she who'd inherited the house, from an aunt who'd married well.

'I've no relations here,' I said. 'Or not to my knowledge.'

Mhairi tilted her head, saying nothing.

'You never can tell,' she said at last, giving me a smile.

We sat in companionable silence, listening to the crackle of the fire, Mhairi's fingers working nimbly. At last, she was ready to sit at the machine. I went to boil the kettle again.

'And you've been in the circle?' she asked, on my return. Her eyes slid up, to gauge my response.

I looked away, not wanting Mhairi to see my face, for fear of what she might read there. I stood to place some more peat on the flames.

'I see you have,' she said simply. 'There's no need to try and hide from me. Whatever you've done, or thought, it'll be no different than for the rest of us.'

I looked over my shoulder at her.

'And you've wriggled through the little hole, I shouldn't wonder!'

Seeing my face, she clucked her tongue.

'There's no need to be so secretive about it. We've all done it. All the lassies on Eirig. Sit you down and I'll tell you.'

I did as she bid, though I looked into the fire rather than in Mhairi's direction. Her eyes were too knowing, and I wasn't ready to reveal all that shamed me.

'It was the first laird that began the tradition. Come our thirteenth year, all lassies are taken to the circle, to pass through the sacred stone. It's said to enhance fertility, not just for the lassies themselves but for all creatures on the island. No doubt, the laird would have suggested pushing the sheep through if they'd have fitted!'

I allowed myself to look up and saw that her face was nothing but merry.

'You needn't look so terrified,' she admonished. 'The sacred stone gives you knowledge of yourself, that's all. It's a little different for each person, but we share the same longing. There's no shame in it. Without the longing, how would we survive?'

I managed a half-hearted smile.

'Samhain is approaching, of course, and that's a bit more serious. Reverend McTavish used to turn a blind eye. He knew that some things on the island weren't for changing, no matter what he preached in the pulpit. Perhaps best that there's none to take his place, for it could be most inconvenient.'

I'd heard of the old Samhain rituals, of sweeping out the house with a besom broom, and the bonfires over which people used to jump, to cleanse the old, and welcome the new. It was a festival of light born out of darkness, of encouraging life from the dormant earth.

'We do things properly here,' continued Mhairi, turning the hand wheel to set the thread through the bobbin. 'There's the mumming, of course. The men do like to dress up and go giving us a scare. Impersonating the souls of the dead, you see. Come to revisit us. The veil's thin on that night, between this world and the next. Every home sets extra places at the table, so they know they're welcome.'

The room was warm enough, but a shiver crossed my back.

'The women play their part too. We're the most

important, you could say, for doesn't life spring from us?

Mhairi's foot worked the peddle as she spoke, the needle moving in and out of the fabric.

'The rams are essential too, but we only need a few of those. It's the number of ewes that's important.'

'The rams?' I asked, frowning.

'Yes, the rams!' Mhairi shook her head. 'Menfolk! Those with the seed! Didn't your mother tell you anything?'

My cheeks warmed a little. If she only knew what I thought of when I lay under the covers. I knew more than my mother had ever told me. I rose to pour us more tea.

The warmth of the room was making me sleepy. 'Sorry,' I said, stifling a yawn. 'My dreams have been waking me.' I lowered my eyes to the rim of my cup.

'Dreams, is it?' said Mhairi. 'I know a bit about those.' She sat back on her heels to look at me. 'Tell me if you like, and I'll interpret them.'

The blush came fierce upon me at the idea.

'Ah, those sort of dreams…' Mhairi smiled. 'In that case, I'll leave them where they lie.'

She twisted in her seat and took something from her pocket. 'Here,' she said, tossing it to me.

It was an acorn.

'Good fortune,' she explained. 'All the potential of the future tree; all the promise of strength to come.'

To satisfy her, I rubbed its smoothness, and held it in my palm.

'If you like, we can do a bit of foretelling,' said Mhairi. She reached into her other pocket and drew out two hazelnuts, holding one aloft. 'You name the person you desire most, and throw the nut in the fire. If it jumps out, it means they aren't keen on you, but if it roasts quietly, their passion burns as bright as your own.'

She handed me the little nut, whispering to her own and throwing it into the flames. After a moment, it hissed and popped, but stayed within the hearth.

'Ha! I knew it already,' declared Mhairi. 'Go on then,' she prompted, looking over at me. 'You don't need to say it aloud.'

It was a ridiculous game, such as was popular on New Year's Eve. My mother had disapproved of such things, saying they were inappropriate for God-fearing Christians.

At the thought of the names I wanted to say, I felt the heat in my cheek again. I said them anyway, to myself, and cast the nut in the flames. It fell deep, and Mhairi clapped her hands in delight.

'That's desire, right enough,' she proclaimed. 'Burning slow and sure.' She nudged me saucily. 'Just wait,' she said. 'You'll see.'

CHAPTER 10

THAT NIGHT, my dreams took me again to the maze, to pathways pulsing with the heartbeat of a living entity. But, I was no intruder. I was an expected guest, drawn through its arteries, to where the maze wished me to step. As I entered deeper, I heard a low, wailing sob and ran forward, knowing someone to be in distress. I woke to find my covers pushed away, so that I lay chill. It was the cold that had roused me. The night was silent.

I drew the blankets to my neck and wriggled beneath them, rubbing my feet together in an attempt to warm them.

When it began again, I wondered if I'd slipped into dozing. The keening seemed to come through the walls of the house. I closed my eyes, wondering if it would enable me not to hear that long, drawn cry. Was it a child? I'd been in the house a full week and seen none, been told of none.

I couldn't remain in my bed. I swung my feet out, feeling for my slippers, retrieving my dressing gown from the chair. I lit the lamp upon my bedside and slipped into the corridor. The oil was running low and the flame rose no more than an inch; beyond my arm, nothing seemed to exist. I reached out my left hand, to touch what I knew to be there: the wallpaper's texture, coarse under my fingertips, and the edge of the cabinet near my door, upon which stood a small figure of a stag.

When the wail rose once more, I followed, passing empty bedrooms. There was no sound or movement behind the doors. I paused at the last: Mrs McInnes' room. Perhaps she'd already woken and was rising to investigate. I whispered her name, to no reply, then turned the handle. She'd wish me to wake her, surely?

The curtains hadn't been drawn, moonlight silvering the outlines of the room's furniture. The bedcovers had been thrown back, as if hurriedly, left askew upon the bed. She wasn't there.

I stilled myself, hearing too much the heartbeat in my chest. One of the girls, Flora or Shona or

Margaret, had woken from a bad dream. Mrs McInnes had gone to them. There was no need for me to interfere.

The wail fell silent and I resolved to make my way back. I didn't wish Mrs McInnes to find me in her room. It was absurd for me to be wandering the house at this hour, without even proper light to guide me. I might trip and turn my ankle, or happen upon the top of the stairs and lose my footing. My courage had left me.

However, as I reached out once more to follow the wall, the mournful howling surged, louder than ever, drifting to me from the end of the corridor. That way led to the East Wing, where the Laird had his apartments, where I'd been warned not to venture. I'd no wish to investigate. And yet, I couldn't ignore that plaintive weeping.

EVEN BY THE pitiful flame of my lamp I could see that this part of the house was in a neglected state. The air was musty, and the walls damp.

The strangeness of the corridor seemed to make the shadows darker. Stumbling into something, I stubbed my toe through my slippers. Cursing, I raised the light, to see a bucket on the floor, collecting the drip of water from above. There was a chair beside it, the upholstery eaten at the corner. By moths, or mice. With the roof leaking, I wondered how many of the floorboards were rotting.

The crying had ceased again. I had heard nothing for several minutes. I waited, aware of the cold dark at my back, and the unknown dark in front of me. And then I heard a low murmur.

Just ahead, and to my right, a door was ajar, a narrow strip of light emerging. I left my lamp upon the seat and felt my way to the threshold, listening to the soft crooning of a woman, as if urging her child to sleep.

'There, there, my love.'

The woman sitting upon the bed, though her back was turned to me, was unmistakably Mrs McInnes. It was her voice I heard, singing a few snatches of a lullaby. By the light of the lamp upon the bedside cabinet I saw her, leaning over the figure within the bed.

She kissed his forehead and, as she drew back, I saw the face upon the pillow: wan and haggard but with features I recognized, from the painting.

I shrunk away from the door, into the shadows, aware of being where I should not.

CHAPTER 11

MRS CAMERON DIDN'T COME to the house on Monday, feeling under the weather.

'If the boys bring you some game, will you make a stew?' asked Mrs. McInnes.

My chest tightened as they came in, Neas carrying a hare by its feet. I kept my eyes on the turnip I was chopping, attacking it with more vigour.

I'd contrived to avoid them as much as I was able. They took their breakfasts earlier than I, and ate lunch, often, in the barn. It was only at the evening supper that I was obliged to sit across from them at the large table in the kitchen. They would wink, and smile, but said never a word else to trouble me, under their mother's eye. I felt, once, Neas' finger creep to lay upon my thigh, and was obliged to endure his insolent caress before reaching beneath to pinch the back of his hand. Eachainn had a habit of extending his foot, to rub his shin upon mine. It was a childish game: an attempt to make me blush, or exclaim. One I was determined not to play. I would not be teased, like a foolish girl in the schoolyard.

Eachainn placed the limp creature down, and leant his bulk against the edge of the table.

'I've not skinned one before,' I said, clenching hard upon the handle of my knife, and slicing roughly into a carrot. 'I don't think I can.' In my rashness, the blade slipped and nicked the tip of my thumb. I swore and raised it to my mouth, to suck away the pain.

'Then there's something else we can teach you,' said Neas, who'd moved to stand on my other side, close enough that I could smell the earth on him and the ripeness of livestock.

He eased my thumb from my mouth and, for a moment, I expected him to place it into his own, to lick away the bright bead forming. Instead, he lowered my hand to the hare, pressing my palm to its warmth. A droplet of my blood smeared upon its soft brown fur.

'We could cut the head off first,' he said, 'But it's not the cleanest way. We don't want to bloody the table more than's needed.'

Eachainn had taken the jointing knife from the block. I took back my hand as he scraped the edge of the blade around the hare's neck, trimming the fur, to expose the pallid skin.

'Feet next,' he said. 'Just above the joint.'

He pressed the knife firmly through the space where the bones met, and a trickle of red oozed from the wound.

'Now for the fur.'

Taking my hand, he made me bunch the skin of the hare's chest, so that he could make an incision, sliding his finger gently into the cut, working the skin away from the meat.

'That vegetable knife will do for this,' he said, cutting upwards, without puncturing the flesh. He slid two fingers beneath the skin, raising it as he sliced.

'Now for the trickiest part. You need to take your time, lassie. No rushing, or the flesh may be damaged.'

I watched as he cut the skin about the neck. He drew the hare's arms through, then pulled, inch by inch, the hide from the connective tissue. Beneath, the meat was dark red, enclosed by its thin membrane. A final tug, and the hind legs were released.

'Just the tailbone left,' he said, snapping it in one easy stroke.

I felt myself sway and Eachainn stepped closer, taking me under the elbow, turning me towards him. I attempted to focus upon the buttons of his checked shirt: old cotton, worn thin from wear.

'Och,' said Neas, 'And we haven't even taken out the organs yet. Don't worry about the hare, lassie. Its spirit will still run the fields, no matter that we eat it.' I was aware of his breath, stirring lightly the hair beneath my ear. 'Such a pretty thing,' he whispered.

I swayed again, but this time not from the sight of the bare meat. I could feel the heat of him behind me, and the pressure of a muscular thigh, against the back of my own.

Eachainn cupped my face, raising it, giving me the scrape of his jaw as well as the softness of his mouth, urging me to cede to him.

Were it not for the strong hands of his brother upon my waist, I might have fallen. I allowed myself to dissolve within that kiss, conscious all the while of Neas reaching beneath my sweater, to pluck the fabric of my blouse from where it tucked into my skirt, his fingers finding the bare skin of my back.

'Are you like the hare, lassie? Fickle as the moon?

He unbuttoned the skirt, then reached to the front, until his palm lay hot upon my lower belly. I thought of him reaching lower, to cup between my legs, pressing his fingers to where I'd so often done the same, and moaned with the imagining of it.

Eachainn's tongue entered my mouth and his kiss became more urgent, his body harder, the swollen desire of him pushing through his trousers. Neas rubbed against the curve of my buttock.

'Sweet hare,' he whispered again. 'Have you been thinking of us, in the night?'

I COULDN'T HAVE SAID how long she'd been standing there. The kitchen door was open, and she'd made no sound.

When she spoke, her tone was peremptory.

'Now, now, my boys. That's enough, I do believe.'

Eachainn drew away, and Neas too, leaving me to

clutch my skirt. I uttered some sound, of strangulated shame, unable to meet her eye, or theirs.

'I see you're not backward in your courting, boys, but I fear you'll overwhelm Miss Muir. She can hardly be accustomed to such attentions.'

With that, she retired to her parlour.

CHAPTER 12

I WAS unable to shake my sense of indignity, and
awkwardness. Mrs McInnes uttered no judgement,
yet I fancied she became more watchful. I had the
sense of her wanting to say something of impor-
tance, waiting for the right moment.

I left the room whenever Neas, or Eachainn,
entered, but was unable to avoid their proximity
when we gathered for our supper. I hadn't known
that my body was capable of such deception, of
responding so fiercely, despite the objections of my
mind. When a hand strayed to rest upon my leg, I
found my knees parting, rather than pulling away,
and willed for that touch to reach further, to find the
softness of my inner thigh.

I hardly knew what I ate, under that strange

enchantment. My body became disconnected, yet intensely alive to sensation. If I closed my eyes, I could hear Neas' voice, close to my ear, and feel his hands, warm, upon my skin. I could taste the urgency of Eachainn's kiss. The scent of them, the potency of them, lingered. The memory was in my body.

If I were to find myself in the same situation, alone with them, would I behave differently? With their hands beneath my clothing, their mouths on my skin, passing me from one to the other, stripping away propriety as surely as the skin pulled from the hare, I knew I would offer them everything.

My dreams were no longer of an unseen presence. Nor were they simple fantasies of giving my body to a man. Now, they returned me to wander the maze. My flesh felt the pull of pathways. I would enter, and the part of myself I'd too long kept hidden would show itself. I lay naked and, from the shadows of each standing stone, they drew forward. Figures unknown to me, hooded, masked. Held captive by the stone, I had no choice but to open my legs to each in turn. I begged for them to end my torture yet I surrendered, to the rise and swell of their thrusts, eager for more of that exquisite pain.

Waking breathless, my heartbeat echoing their

surging rhythms, the sheets damp with sweat, and my hand pressed insistently to my sex, I trembled with the unbridled sexuality of those dreams. The ghost-print of that torment bloomed and burned, where I had yielded, broken open like ripe fruit, consumed in the dark.

My imagination was a traitor to me, such that I began to doubt my sanity. I no longer recognized myself. I fluttered, trapped in the belly of that monstrous maze. It felt me, I knew, moving inside. Even my evening walks now failed to soothe me. I felt the proximity of the hidden circle and remembered the dark shame of my dreams. With the soft settle of descending dusk, the clench of desire never failed to grip me.

On other nights, the Laird's cries drifted into my dreams from afar. Drawn to follow that low keening, my sleeping-self wandered the house, toes bare on the wooden boards, clad only in my nightgown, until the moans of sorrow baited me outside, for they came not from within those walls, but beyond.

Beneath the hook of the moon, I ran, beckoned forwards, lured towards the swaddled centre of the labyrinth, the grass cool upon the soles of my feet. The cries no longer sounded like those of an old man. They were infant wails, urgent and vulnerable.

Among the shadows, I saw a small figure, a baby, its mouth twisted wet, laying naked upon the flattened surface of the stone. I reached for its pale body but woke, always, before I might lift it to the safety of my arms.

CHAPTER 13

ONE MORNING, I was passing the dining room, where Shona and Margaret were polishing the silver. Our Inverary house had so long been quiet, with just myself and my father, that it was still a novelty to me to come upon others in the house, and to hear their conversation.

They spoke in hushed tones, but loud enough that I was able to hear them from the corridor.

'I'm glad enough that it's not me as has to tend him,' came Shona's voice. You heard him, the other night?'

'Say what you like about her but she cares for him better than most wives would,' Margaret replied. 'She won't let anyone disturb him, for his nerves are all awry.'

'Not just his nerves. It's his mind that's turned,' said Shona.

'I never liked him,' sniffed Margaret. 'I was only fourteen when I came, but it didn't stop him putting himself where he wasn't invited. The Laird's lady was still mistress here then, but he thought nothing of taking liberties.'

'Ha!' said Shona. 'You're not the only one! We're better off with him bedridden, or we'd be having to put up with all sorts!'

I remembered the sallow face I'd seen upon the pillow. It was hard to imagine him as a randy young goat, bothering the housemaids, but I knew enough of men to realize that there was unlikely to be exaggeration in their complaint.

'He's been ill for far too long, and unable to fulfil his duties,' Shona added. 'Everyone knows the Laird has responsibilities to the island. It's time to let another take his place. Samhain is coming and he can't do what must be done.'

Their voices dropped, so that I was unable to hear more of what was said, though I leaned as far into the doorway as I dared, without risking being seen.

A movement down the hall alerted me to the arrival of Mrs McInnes, seeking me out. I was obliged to pretend that I'd been straightening a picture on the wall, then turned, and hurried to meet her, before she might overhear anything from the room at which I'd been eavesdropping.

She wished to show me the storerooms in the West Wing, to which we carried some old mirrors. We'd been placing the best of the furnishings in what would become our guest apartments.

As we entered its long corridor, I thought of what I'd seen: of Mrs McInnes and the Laird, in the opposite wing of the house.

She took a key from her collection to unlock the door, though I could see no reason to keep the contents of the room secure. There was nothing but the oldest furniture: chairs with broken seats and tattered upholstery. The spiders had been at work, and there was scratching in the skirting. Mice, for sure. If something of value existed amongst these disused items, it was well hidden.

'There's a painting here that might do for our 'Heather Room', if only I can find it,' called Mrs McInnes, moving further among the clutter.

Several travelling trunks were stacked against the wall: good ones, of leather and wood. I crouched to try the lid on the largest. It wasn't locked. There was fabric inside, in purple and orange, and some pieces of sheepskin. Pulling them aside, I almost dropped the lid. A dark-eyed face leered out at me, its teeth bared in a grin. It was hideous, more animal than human, but was just a mask after all, not some demon come to judge me.

I turned it over, and found a small rod beneath, trimmed with ribbon, topped by a ring of bells. I realized then that these must be costumes: those of Mhairi's mummers, I guessed.

Mrs McInnes still had her back to me, bending in her own pursuit, but I decided to look no further, closing the lid with a quiet click.

I'D NOTICED that Mrs McInnes not only took the Laird all his meals, but would carry tea to his rooms several times through the day: her special tea, such as she made for us often. I'd thought nothing of her attentiveness. She'd served in the house all her adult life. He was her master.

It was quite by chance that I came to her parlour as she was setting her tray and saw her take a bottle from the desk of her drawer. A small brown bottle, from which she shook four drops into the pot. I retreated, so that she might not know I'd seen her.

No doubt, the medicine had been prescribed by Dr McBane. The Laird was confined to his rooms, in some debilitating state, as Mrs Cameron had explained to me. I guessed the bottle contained an opiate, to help him sleep.

I coughed as I stepped forward, and caught a glimpse of the bottle disappearing into her pocket.

'Miss Muir, how quietly you step.' She lifted the tray. 'As you see, I'm on my way upstairs, to sit with the Laird for a while.'

I stood for some moments after she'd departed. The drawer from which she'd taken the bottle had not been fully closed. A boldness overtook me, so rather than sliding it shut, I pulled the drawer open further.

Inside was her accounting book, fountain pen, and chequebook. Several withdrawals had been made recently. I recognized the payees as well-known department stores in Glasgow and Edin-burgh. One cheque lay ready to be posted, made out to a haberdashery in Oban. It was signed by Mrs McInnes herself, rather than by the Laird. How greatly he must trust her, to allow her access to his banking account.

Beneath was an envelope, unsealed. I unfolded the paper and found not a cheque this time but a letter, addressed to a firm of law, in Fort William. It took but a moment to scan the page, and to look at the second. I'd only seen a will of last testament once before, but recently enough that I recognized the phrases and knew their import. My father had left me not only the house but a modest sum; I'd been his sole beneficiary.

The ink was barely dry on the page, for it had been signed only the day before. The house, estate and all assets were to be managed by Mrs McInnes on the Laird's passing, until her sons reached the age of twenty-five, when the men would inherit jointly. The official title, of Laird, it appeared, would pass to Neas. Such was the benefit of his having been born a few minutes before his brother.

I scanned to the bottom, where the Laird's signature had been placed. The hand was far from steady, but the result was legible, and had been witnessed by the very two I'd eavesdropped upon that morning: Shona and Margaret.

CHAPTER 14

IT MATTERED little that I did my best to stay away from Neas and Eachainn, for events conspired against me. A few days previously, I'd watched them leave, setting off to drive the larger part of the sheep into the village. From there, the boats would take them to the mainland. The McInnes men were responsible for fetching home the best price the auction could summon.

However, only three days passed before Mrs McInnes told me they were due back on the morning tide.

'You'll take the cart to fetch them? It would be such a help. The horses know the track. You need do nothing more but sit atop, then await the boat at the harbour.'

I'd visited the stables rarely, fearful of finding myself in company I wished to avoid, but I knew the horses were steady creatures. I'd taken them carrot ends and an apple or two. They'd always nuzzled my hand good-naturedly.

I set off in good time, fearing some mishap on the journey. Despite the placidity of the two fillies pulling the cart, I remained anxious. We passed the way that Mhairi had brought me, some weeks ago. It seemed that I'd been on Eirig a lifetime.

I looked up at the walls of yew as I descended the hill, and felt an urge to stop the cart. The strange significance of the circle for the women of the island continued to haunt me. My thoughts turned often to what lay within the maze. Its dark shadow wound about me, waking and sleeping.

However, I feared being late, and made myself continue, casting only one backward look before I entered the shade of arching trees.

I need not have worried, for the boat was still some way out when I reached the harbour. I sat, watching its approach, imagining how Mhairi must have done the same on the day she collected me.

After some minutes, however, I found that I was terribly thirsty. In my anxiety, I'd left without bringing anything to drink, and there were no clouds and little wind that day, to soften the warmth of the sun.

The school, I'd been told, was only a short distance beyond the harbour, so I tethered the horses, setting off to beg a glass of water. I found it easily enough, from the shouts of the children, playing in the yard. They made sufficient noise, though there were only eight of them. Two girls turned a skipping rope, singing a song to keep the rhythm, while the third jumped, plaits flying. Five boys were kicking a ball, though it was unclear where their goal was situated.

The schoolmistress met me at the gate, introducing herself as Miss Mackley, asking how I found Eirig, and if I was comfortable at Dorchadas House. She invited me to visit her anytime, eager for a visitor with more to share than Eirig gossip.

'Tell me about Inverary, when you have the time,' she urged.

I left her with a cheerful wave, glad at having made a new friend: one with whom I believed I'd find much in common. I fear I distracted her from her duties, for we chatted more than half an hour before I took my farewell.

'I've a mind to see the church, while I'm at this end of the island. Is it close?' I asked. If I were quick,

I'd have time, surely. I'd no wish to sit waiting at the harbour, like some love-struck female.

Miss Mackey directed me.

'It's but a few minutes. It'll be unlocked. There's a hole in the roof, I believe, where the birds do tend to fly in, so be careful where you sit,' she warned.

The building was forlorn, like a lover cast off, no longer wanted. I stood a moment under the lychgate, looking across the churchyard. Inside, the leaves had blown in. The pews were dusty and the air damp. It was difficult to imagine a thriving congregation, gathering to sing their hymns and send up their prayers. Nevertheless, that particular feeling of majestic stillness, as all churches seem to have, remained.

As I left the porch, returning to the sunlight, I heard them: a woman's girlish squeal, followed by a voice of lower tone. Not far away, behind the church.

Taking the path that rounded the building, I saw them almost at once; two broad backs and the bending figure of Mhairi, her skirts raised to her waist.

I was afraid to move. Better not to look, nor listen, yet I could not bring myself to leave. I crouched, peering from behind a headstone.

Neas' fingers dug deep into the flesh of her hips, holding her to his thrusts.

'You're too rough,' she complained, then caught her breath.

'Kneel still and abide your tupping,' scolded Eachainn, unbuckling his trousers. He stroked himself, and Mhairi raised her head, to take him in her mouth, drawing back and forth upon his length.

'That's it, little ewe,' he said, placing his hand on her hair. 'I've milk to give ye if ye suck well enough.'

I crawled away, through the grass.

When they returned, I would say that I'd been all the while at the schoolhouse, with Miss Mackley.

CHAPTER 15

Neas took the reins on our journey back to the house, with Eachainn lying in the rear. I sat on the upper seat, with Neas' leg pressed warm to my thigh. The sweat of the sexual act hung heavy on his body.

As we began to cross the heathland, I wondered if they'd stop the cart in some quiet place. I'd be powerless to stop them, no matter what they wished to do. My mouth grew dry at the thought of it. Would they lay me in the back, or take me to the side of the road? They'd be too impatient to be gentle. It would be quick, and rough.

Neither spoke, Neas looking only ahead at the road, and Eachainn closing his eyes in the back.

When we entered the tunnel of arching branches, my breath became tight in my chest. This would be the place. No one would see them. We'd be hidden. They might do as they liked, without fear of being caught. I resolved to unbutton my blouse rather than have it torn. I'd make it easy for them, and perhaps it would hurt less.

I'd thought only of a woman lying on her back for the act, but they might ask me to kneel, as Mhairi had done, like the cows in the field, letting the bull mount them. They'd take turns to thrust between my legs. I pictured Neas unbuckling his trousers and ordering me to take him in my mouth, as Mhairi had done. Would it taste as it smelled?

Where I sat became damp as I waited. That would help, surely, the wetness? It would ease their movement.

It was with some surprise that I saw the house before us. The journey had passed quickly, my mind distracted by the pawing of the creature within me. As I descended from the cart, I felt shame, for I could not deny the ache of my disappointment.

CHAPTER 16

THAT NIGHT, I dreamt of being pressed facedown into the hay. It scratched my naked belly and breasts as they lay upon my back. How heavy they were, pushing my legs apart. I felt them both, nudging their cocks against my buttocks, squeezing the breath from my body. I cried out as they invaded me and smelt them still when I woke.

My door had swung open, allowing a draught to sweep across the room and find me in my bed. Rising to close it, I looked out into the corridor. It was dark, of course. I had no lamp, and could see nothing. There was no movement, no sound, and yet I felt a certain stir in the air. Despite the chill, I stood for some moments, listening. There were voices, somewhere in the house.

I cannot say what made me don my dressing gown and light the lamp. My feet took me where they'd gone before, to the end of the passage and into the East Wing. I leaned forward, into the gap between frame and door. As before, Mrs McInnes was bent over the figure within the bed.

'There, there, my love. It's time now. Time to close your eyes.'

There was no spoken reply, but I heard movement, and a muffled cry, soon deadened.

'Shhh, now. Don't struggle,' urged the voice, in the same subdued tones.

As she sat back, I saw that she'd been pressing down upon a pillow. She lifted it, to stroke the cheek of that poor face, its mouth slack.

I realized then what I'd witnessed and the blackness threatened to unbalance me, as if the floor was no longer solid beneath my feet.

I remembered my father's last night. Had his legs twitched beneath the blankets as the Laird's had done?

How I found my way to my room, or what noise I made, I cannot recall.

I fell through my door and applied the lock, dragging the small armchair from its place by the hearth, to block the entrance. For what remained of the night, I lay awake, expecting the handle to turn.

By the time dawn entered between the curtains, I'd made my decision. Mrs McInnes would deny having ended the Laird's life, and her word would stand above my own. My accusations would be scorned. They'd tell me that I'd been dreaming. I almost doubted myself, but for the tenderness of a bruise upon my hip, where I'd caught my side against a cabinet in the dark corridor.

There was no telephone, though Eirig had an old telegraph machine, inside the postal office. I might send a message to the mainland, alerting the police, but I knew it would be foolhardy. The postmistress would waste little time in passing along my action to Dorchadas House, and what position would I then be in? Even were the police to come, what would I say? That I believed Mrs McInnes had murdered the Laird? After years of nursing him?

She'd done it for her boys, I knew, but perhaps also for herself.

Long nights I'd sat beside my father, listening to his laboured breathing. So many times, I'd imagined taking the cushion from the chair. How easy it was, in the end. Only cowardice had stayed my hand from acting sooner. My guilt was between me and my maker, and I'd answer for it in the hereafter. The doctor had pronounced a natural death, remarking his surprise at my father's strength, enduring far longer than might have been expected. He praised my dutiful care. I'd deceived him, but not myself.

I'd carry, now, the burden not only of my own sin, but that of Mrs McInnes too.

CHAPTER 17

Mrs McInnes gathered everyone to the kitchen, to announce the Laird's passing. The news was met with composure.

'A blessing it is,' said Mrs Cameron. 'I'd not wish to linger so long myself.'

I thought of telling her the truth, but I knew it would be wasted breath. Even were she to believe me, she'd think it fortunate that the poor man was out of his misery.

Margaret and Shona exchanged a look and said nothing. Only Flora's eyes were wet.

Having given Neas and Eachainn the task of bringing down the Laird, to lay him in one of the unused downstairs rooms, Mrs McInnes went straight to her parlour.

'Letters for the solicitor who oversees the legality of the estate, and to call the doctor to us,' she explained. 'A death certificate must be submitted.'

She looked me clear in the eye, as if defying me to question her. If she suspected my seeing what had occurred the previous night, she gave no indication. I should have feared her, or felt revulsion. But what a hypocrite I'd be, for wasn't the same stain upon my own soul? I was no innocent. I'd ended life as knowingly as she.

Our shared sin only drew me closer.

CHAPTER 18

'YOU CAN HELP me carve the turnips if you like,' said Mrs Cameron. 'We'll put them in the window.'

I was peeling apples for the pie and hadn't been concentrating as I should, lost in my own thoughts. Was I safe, in this house? Mrs McInnes had watched me carefully that first day, and the next. By the time the doctor came, she'd settled back almost into her old self. I'd caught her singing, in her parlour, after Dr McBane had left. I understood. A burden had been lifted. She was truly her own mistress now.

'Mrs McInnes will be setting extra places, so they can join us while we sup.'

'Sorry, Mrs Cameron, who's that? Who's coming?'

'Och, lassie!' said Mrs Cameron, 'The spirits, o' course! Do they not celebrate Samhain in Inverary?'

They did not, I thought. Or, at least, not in the same way as upon Eirig. The pastor at All Saints' Church would hardly approve.

'And at the head of the table our beloved Laird, rest his soul. He'd been so long confined, and shrunk to a shadow of his former self. You should have seen him, Miss Muir. He was a fine figure of a man. Mrs McInnes did a marvellous job keeping the place running while he faded in his bed. No man should endure that indignity. Better to go in your sleep, I always think.'

I nodded. There was truth in what she said, even though it wasn't the whole truth.

My thoughts wandered again, this time to Neas and Eachainn. They'd continued in their duties, showing neither grief nor elation, ignoring me for the most part, such that I wondered if their mother had warned them against misbehaviour. Did she fear I'd leave?

I remained uncertain what to do for the best. The plumber was due to arrive the very next week, and the electrician had promised to come before the worst of the winter weather made a crossing difficult.

'Here,' said Mrs Cameron, picking up one of the apples. 'Skin it in one long strip, then toss the peel over your shoulder. We'll look at the shape, and see if it forms the first letter of your admirer's name.'

I shook my head. 'If you can spare me, I'll take a walk. There's an hour or so before it gets dark.'

'Don't be too long,' she replied. 'Return before sunset, for that's when we'll begin.'

Apple bobbing, I supposed, and other games. All foolishness, and I wasn't in the mood.

I was some way up the hill before I realized the path I'd taken. Ahead loomed the tall, dark wall of yew, and I felt the familiar tug within my body. I paused at the archway, remembering the euphoria of that first day, of my feelings of freedom, and of defiance. The same urgency nagged at me now. It was as if this place sought my presence, as if it had called to me, from afar, bringing me here for its own purpose. Something was waiting for me within the maze, enticing me to enter.

Reaching the end of the first passageway, taking the paths as I had before, I caught sight of a flash of skirt.

'Follow me,' whispered a voice, soft and feminine, on the other side of the hedge. She was ahead of me, singing softly: an old Scots ballad.

O where have you been, my dearest love,

This long day and mair?

I've yearned for you, my bonny love,

Grant me your comfort as before.

I found a shoe discarded on the path, and a woollen shawl. Around the next corner, a skirt and blouse lay as they'd been thrown. The voice grew bolder, and there could be no mistaking the lewdness of the ditty.

He turned me right and round about,
And said 'Now shall ye see;
I've an oak to bury in your streaming fount.
My seed I'll give to thee.

Only another turn and I'd reach the centre. On the path lay more clothing. Under-things: worsted stockings and a petticoat. I knew whose voice it was. I knew who'd be waiting for me.

He drew his sword to the very hilt,
And buried his fight with toil,

He near did break me all in twain,
  As he sank beneath my soil.

She must have been cold, yet lay as if bathed in the sun's warmth, at ease upon her back, her bare body elongated upon the central stone. Her hand rested between her parted thighs. She hummed the tune, now, as if only to herself.

I'd seen my own body naked but never that of another woman. I found that I couldn't look away. Her belly was rounded, though the rest of her was as slim as ever. She'd concealed it cleverly beneath her clothes, but I guessed she was four months gone. It was no wonder she'd been in need of making a new dress.

Mhairi's voice carried again, but in a different song now: an ululation to accompany the bucking of her hips against her fingers. It ended in a low keening wail, her hand pressed hard between her legs. My own had moved downwards, inside my coat, pushing against the fabric of my dress.

She sat up and looked at me. 'Miss Muir,' she whispered, as if to beckon me. 'Iris.' She laughed then. A woman's laugh. One of knowing.

I fled back, the way I'd come.

CHAPTER 19

THERE WAS blood on the doorstep on my return, more black than red in the half-light. I stepped over carefully, to enter the kitchen.

'It's from the rooster,' said Mrs Cameron, chivvying me into the warmth. 'To protect the house.' She wiped her hands on her apron. 'It's only natural that the poor spirits of the departed should want to find shelter, but not all are welcome.'

'Quite so,' said Mrs McInnes, joining us. 'Miss Muir, you'll help me lay the table?'

I watched her counting out the plates. One for us all and several more.

'The veil is thin between the living and the dead tonight,' she continued. 'May the soul of our departed laird, and his good wife and wee son, rest in peace.'

I wondered at her speaking the words so calmly.

'Perhaps your father will find you tonight, Miss Muir,' she added. 'I'll set a place, in his honour, and for your mother, too.'

After a moment's hesitation, I nodded my assent, though Mrs McInnes' conscience seemed to be untroubled, my own pricked me.

'You have the look of him. I knew you for his as soon as I saw you.' She patted my arm. 'You know the truth, I think.'

Mrs Cameron turned from the stove, listening.

'As soon as I saw the correspondence from you, I wondered...' said Mrs McInnes. 'It was the year Donald turned twenty-three that he left Eirig. I'd held a torch for him since I was a girl.'

I frowned. My father had always been vague about where he'd lived before coming to Inverary.

'He sent letters, the first months he was away, asking me to join him, but I was too young. My mother would never have allowed it. By the time I'd the courage to run away, I'd missed my chance. One of the fishermen brought the news. Donald was to wed some other girl.'

I sat down abruptly at the table, memories of my

father returning. He'd been so frail at the end, it was hard to imagine him in his youth.

'You're of the island, Iris. It's in your blood.'

'And the rest of the family?' I asked, wishing now to know everything. 'I must have relatives here.'

She inclined her head. ''Twas your own family that lived up from the beach,' said Mrs McInnes. 'The Muirs had the worst of it.'

'But some, surely? I must have relations here?'

'Aye, you do,' she conceded. 'But none close. Mhairi's mother was a cousin of yours, so you're related there. We're a tight community, so everyone is related in some way, but none now bear the name of Muir.'

'Only me,' I answered.

Could I grieve for grandparents I'd never met, for aunts and uncles and cousins? I'd never know them. I'd arrived upon Eirig too late for that.

I shivered again with the knowledge that something had called me here.

I'd wanted to escape, and had been brought all the way back, to where I rightfully belonged.

CHAPTER 20

'DRINK YOUR TEA,' said Mrs McInnes. 'I've made it stronger tonight. See if you can sleep. There'll be a bit of noise, and the mummers can be so crude. You don't need to hear all that. The best part of Samhain begins after midnight. I'll come and get you, don't worry. You won't miss out.'

I looked out the window from my bedroom. People had begun arriving from the village, holding lanterns aloft. I pushed up the sash. Someone was playing a pennywhistle, cavorting to their own playful melody. Quite a few had been drinking. The men were shouting in that way men do when they've imbibed more than's good for them, as they chased the girls, to take a playful fondle.

My eyesight wasn't good in the dark. It was hard

for me to focus, but something dark hung in the air, a deeper black than the shadows.

I put my hands on the ledge and felt the roughness of the wood. Its strength had been taken by the weather, and the frame was rotting. I'd add it to the list of things to repair. The house couldn't be left to fall into decay. It was my home, wasn't it? I wasn't going back to Inverary. I'd wasted years but, here, I'd found purpose. I was needed.

My eyes were already closing as I heard the antler horns blowing. Neas and Eachainn would be out there. I wondered how many girls they'd kiss. Too many, and never quite enough.

I WAS STILL DROWSY when I heard Mrs McInnes' voice at my pillow. 'We're ready for you, my dear.' She shook my shoulder. 'You're our guest of honour.'

Raising me from the bed, she brought my slippers to my feet. As she guided me down the corridor, I realized that she wore her woollen cape, while I had only my nightgown, though she'd wrapped a shawl about my shoulders. I thought of the warm dress I'd left folded over my chair, and my own coat upon its hook. However, Mrs McInnes' grip under my elbow was firm, and I was content to be led. I couldn't summon enough concern to protest.

It was hard for me to judge the distance between the stairs but, at last, we reached the hallway. She placed a wreath of flowers on my head, before opening the door. 'They're waiting, you see. All waiting. Just for you.'

It was quiet outside, but for the distant striking of a drum. We followed the pool of yellow cast by our lamp; ahead, on the hill, there was a glow from within the maze.

'I'm the guest of honour,' I repeated. My lips felt strangely numb.

'That's right,' said Mrs McInnes, leading me through the entrance to the maze. 'No need to be afraid.'

Even had she let go her hold, I would have continued forward, my pulse called by the hollow throb of the bodhrán drum. With each footstep, its resonance grew. Then, we turned the final corner, and I saw them.

There were so many gathered inside the circle. It seemed that everyone from the island was present. And how clever were their masks: fish and cockerels, sheep, hares and cows. All the creatures of Eirig.

Some wore tunics, but not black, as I'd dreamed. They were white, tied with purple sashes.

Two wore masks with long, curling ram horns. Where the eyes were cut out was the glint of their own.

'The goddess Nicneven is within you,' whispered Mrs McInnes. 'She'll protect and guide, as the Laird's heirs worship you. It's their sacred duty, and yours now, Iris.'

I knew the broadness of their shoulders, and the muscles upon their arms. Each was naked but for the fleece about his waist.

'Take the seed,' said Mrs McInnes, removing the shawl and lifting the nightdress from my head. 'Bring fruitfulness to your own body, and to all the creatures of our island.'

They carried me to the stone, and I felt no hardness behind my back.

As if I'm on grass.

The fleece tickled between my legs as the first ram leant over me, warm on my belly as he thrust, to the pound of the drum and the chant of the animal circle.

Gabh an sìol

Fàs an sìol

116

Ag àrach an sìol
Breith an sìol

I held my breath as he pushed himself deep, thrusting to where I'd never reached.

My moans of pleasure sounded as if they were coming from far away; from the mouth of some other woman, bolder and more brazen than I could ever be.

So many eyes, watching, and all for me.

When he withdrew, my thighs were wet. As the second entered me, I gasped, but not from pain, or fear. I pushed back against his insistence, and was gratified to hear a returning groan of pleasure from behind the mask.

I found I wished only for more.

CHAPTER 21

HOW STRANGE I FELT, in the dim dawn of that late autumn morning. I'd woken to the click of the closing door, beneath familiar blankets, the green sprig curtain still drawn against the first light. The cast of the room was unchanged, with its simple furniture, and lingering smell of peat. All was as it had ever been, but I was not the same woman.

I winced, on pulling myself up against the pillows. Someone had lit the fire, and left tea at my bedside. It was welcome, hot and sweet.

Deep between my legs, I throbbed. To the touch of my hand, my breasts were tender. Beneath me, my nightdress was damp.

I'd yielded to a force I could not have resisted. I should have felt myself shamed, but I did not.

I eased to the edge of the bed and placed my feet on the floor. My slippers were waiting, sitting as they always did, neatly together, though there was grass upon them. Between my toes, the mud had dried.

Whatever darkness the past held, it had gathered to propel me here: the death of my mother, my own ending of my father's suffering.

I rose to draw back the curtains, taking in the russet heathland, beneath the wide sky of violet-grey. The rising wall of the maze no longer intimidated me. I knew its secrets.

Gabh an sìol.
Fàs an sìol.

The words of the Gaelic chant echoed through my memory.

Take the seed.
Grow the seed.

I wondered how many generations of island folk had sung those words, every Samhain.

Eirig held deeper significance than I'd ever imagined. Its landscapes were woven through my family history. Its ancestral voices whispered to my blood. The island's seed was within me, connecting me to every rock and to the roots of the trees. I fancied I could hear the shiver of a snake in the grass, and the sound of each blade lengthening.

In this wild place, my own wildness had grown steadily, had found its way out. Here, where no one judged. No twitching tongues; only shared knowledge.

I poured hot water from the pitcher into the washstand basin, and splashed my face clean.

EPILOGUE

'YOU WRITE THE ADVERTISEMENT, MY DEAR,' she says, passing the ink, and the same blue notepaper on which she wrote to me. It seems so long ago. 'We need more hands to help. We'll be so busy, when the first guests arrive.'

Over the winter, my belly has grown; I can't climb ladders anymore, but there are other things to keep me busy.

Neas still squeezes my knee beneath the table. 'Growing our wee bairn, little hare,' he whispers, giving my ear a nip.

Eachainn rubs my lower back, which aches when I sit too long.

I think of them in my bed, and smile.

Mhairi will deliver first, of course, just before the lambs come.

'New blood,' says Mrs McInnes. 'That's what Eirig needs.'

GAELIC TRANSLATIONS

Tigh Dorchadas - House of Darkness

Gabh an sìol - Take the seed

Fàs an sìol - Grow the seed

Ag àrach an sìol - Nurture the seed

Breith an sìol - Birth the seed

ALSO BY EMMANUELLE DE MAUPASSANT

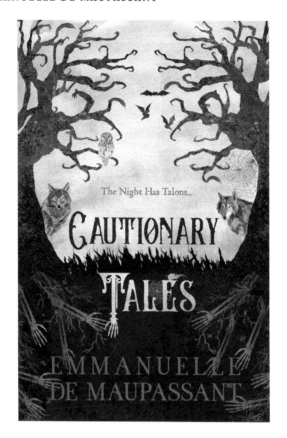

Cautionary Tales

The boundaries between the everyday and the unearthly are snakeskin-thin. The trees have eyes and the night has talons. Demons, drawn by the perfume of human vice and wickedness, lurk with intents malicious and capricious.

Tread carefully, for the dark things best left behind in the forest may seep under your door and sup with you. The lover at your window or in your bed may have the scent of your death already on their breath.

'Funny, brutal, and irreverent' – Bustle.com

Twelve tales inspired by Eastern European and Russian superstitions and folklore; darkly delicious imaginings for the adult connoisseur of bedtime stories.

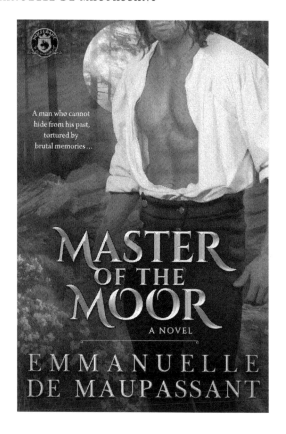

Master of the Moor

A man tortured by brutal memories...
A woman determined to safeguard her liberty...
After more than twenty years in exile, Mallon de Wolfe—formidable, handsome, and with a shard of ice where his heart should be—is returning to Dartmoor.

A place vast, barren and perilous.

A place where secrets refuse to remain buried.

Mallon has vowed to conquer the betrayals of his youth, but faces new danger as his attraction grows for the mysterious Countess Rosseline.

Haunted by scandal and the shame of her bloodline, the newly-widowed Countess is without scruples. She needs a husband capable of securing her status, even if it means resorting to deceit and entrapment. Is Mallon's desire for her too intoxicating to be denied, no matter what the price—and can either escape the poisonous dominion of their past?

ABOUT THE AUTHOR

Emmanuelle de Maupassant lives with her husband (maker of tea and fruit cake) and her hairy pudding terrier (connoisseur of squeaky toys and bacon treats). She has lived on five continents, but her heart remains in the Highlands.

You can find her on Twitter and Facebook
Send her a hello. Tag her in a review.
Give her a wave, and she'll wave back.

For behind the scenes chat, join Emmanuelle's Facebook 'Boudoir' group.

www.emmanuelledemaupassant.com

Melissa Coffey is a writer, editor and poet, residing in Melbourne, Australia. She holds a BA (Hons) in theatre studies. Through her fiction and non-fiction writing, she engages strongly with themes of the feminine experience.

Her memoir short story "Motherlines", published in Australian anthology **Stew and Sinkers** (Stringybark Press 2013), was awarded Highly Commended, and her feminist creative essay "Body Com/positions" features in literary journal **Etchings** ("Visual Eyes"#12, Ilura Press 2013). Most recently, her poem "Sweat / Shop" appears in the March 2018 issue of **Not Very Quiet**, an online poetry journal featuring international women poets.

After many years interpreting play-texts as a theatre director, Melissa now applies those skills to fiction, deepening the "theatre on the page", and enhancing the writer's voice through developmental editing. She unexpectedly fell into developmental editing whilst writing and publishing under a pseudonym, and has worked with authors on numerous novellas, novelettes and around fifty short stories via her pseudonym. **Dorchadas House** is her first major editing project under her real name.

Melissa's short stories, flash fiction and poetry focusing on female sexuality have been published under her pseudonym in numerous international anthologies and **Cosmopolitan U.K.**

Currently, Melissa is diving into several projects exploring the potential of myth and fairy tale to interrogate, subvert and re-imagine the feminine experience.

Connect with Melissa
On Twitter
On Facebook

Printed in Great Britain
by Amazon